This is the
Pharaoh Sennapod,
and his cat, Crusher
of Worms.

And these two are Jelly
and Grimstone. They're
determined to steal the
Pharaoh's treasure.

But first they have to get out of prison ...

Are you feeling silly enough to read more?

Jeremy Strong once worked in a bakery, putting the jam into three thousand doughnuts every night. Now he puts the jam in stories instead, which he finds much more exciting. At the age of three, he fell out of a first-floor bedroom window and landed on his head. His mother says that this damaged him for the rest of his life and refuses to take any responsibility. He loves writing stories because he says it is 'the only time you alone have complete control and can make anything happen'. His ambition is to make you laugh (or at least snuffle). Jeremy Strong lives near Bath with his wife, Gillie, four cats and a flying cow.

LAUGH YOUR SOCKS OFF WITH

Jeremy STRONG

Let's Do the PHARAOH!

Illustrated by

Rowan Clifford

PUFFIN

PUFFIN BOOKS

Published by the Penguin Group
Penguin Books Ltd, 80 Strand, London WC2R 0RL, England
Penguin Group (USA) Inc., 375 Hudson Street, New York, New York 10014, USA
Penguin Group (Canada), 90 Eglinton Avenue East, Suite 700, Toronto, Ontario, Canada M4P 2Y3
(a division of Pearson Penguin Canada Inc.)
Penguin Ireland, 25 St Stephen's Green, Dublin 2, Ireland (a division of Penguin Books Ltd)
Penguin Group (Australia), 250 Camberwell Road, Camberwell, Victoria 3124, Australia
(a division of Pearson Australia Group Pty Ltd)
Penguin Books India Pvt Ltd, 11 Community Centre, Panchsheel Park, New Delhi – 110 017, India
Penguin Group (NZ), 67 Apollo Drive, Rosedale, North Shore 0632, New Zealand
(a division of Pearson New Zealand Ltd)
Penguin Books (South Africa) (Pty) Ltd, 24 Sturdee Avenue, Rosebank, Johannesburg 2196, South Africa

Penguin Books Ltd, Registered Offices: 80 Strand, London WC2R 0RL, England

puffinbooks.com

First published in Puffin Books 2004
This edition published 2009 for The Book People Ltd,
Hall Wood Avenue, Haydock, St Helens, WA11 9UL
1

Text copyright © Jeremy Strong, 2004
Illustrations copyright © Rowan Clifford, 2004
All rights reserved

The moral right of the author and illustrator has been asserted

Set in Baskerville MT
Made and printed in England by Clays Ltd, St Ives plc

British Library Cataloguing in Publication Data
A CIP catalogue record for this book is available from the British Library

ISBN: 978-0-141-32793-8

www.greenpenguin.co.uk

Penguin Books is committed to a sustainable future
for our business, our readers and our planet.
The book in your hands is made from paper
certified by the Forest Stewardship Council.

This is for Daisy

Contents

1 The Queen of Where?

The Pharaoh Sennapod, High King and Ruler of 27 Templeton Drive, sat in front of the mirror and gazed back at himself with a pleased smile. He also happened to be High King and Ruler of Upper and Lower Egypt, but that had been four and a half thousand years earlier. Nowadays he led a rather quieter life with Mr and Mrs Lightspeed and their children, Carrie and Ben.

He was a real Pharaoh, from the almost forgotten Four Fifths Dynasty, and because nobody was supposed to utter his real name, he was also called He Whose Name Shall Rumble Down The Ages.

'Your eyeliner is on crooked,' Carrie pointed out.

'Do you dare criticize the Lord of all Egypt?' grunted Sennapod.

'Yes.' Carrie was quite used to Senny trying to throw his weight about. She didn't care if he was Arch-Emperor of the Entire Universe, he wasn't going to boss her around. After all, she was fifteen, and no sane person tries to boss a fifteen-year-old girl about.

The pair of them were sitting at Carrie's dressing table, putting on their make-up. It was something that Carrie was still not quite used to. The idea of men in make-up seemed pretty weird to Carrie, but her younger brother Ben had told her that even the poorest Ancient Egyptian men wore make-up – at least for special occasions: parties, barbecues, raves, clubbing, that sort of thing.

'The Ancient Egyptians did not go clubbing,' snorted Carrie.

'Of course they did. They had musicians and dancing and all that stuff.'

'Yeah, but not clubbing.'

'It was the same sort of thing,' Ben insisted. 'Loads of people dancing to loud music and looking stupid, like you.'

'I do not look stupid when I dance.'

'I didn't mean you look stupid when you dance,' said Ben, moving in for the kill. 'I meant, you look stupid all the time.'

Carrie leapt up from her chair, trying to grab him, but Sennapod growled at both of them. 'Must you behave like young jackals?' he demanded.

'Ben must, he is one,' snapped Carrie. 'Anyhow, it just feels odd having you sitting next to me shoving my make-up all over your face. I wish you'd buy your own.'

'I am the Pharaoh. I do what I wish. But you are not an Ancient Egyptian, Carrie, so why do you use make-up?'

'That's easy,' snorted Ben. 'If she didn't, she'd scare people to death because she's so ugly.'

Carrie could scare people to death? Sennapod was impressed. Even *he* didn't possess that sort of power and he was a living god, as he frequently told everyone. 'Is this true?' he asked.

'Of course it isn't. Never believe anything

Ben says. If you must know, I'm preparing for a competition.' Carrie fetched a teen mag from her bed and passed it across. A whole page was devoted to the competition.

☆ ☆ ☆ **FAB PRIZES!** ☆ ☆ ☆

ARE YOU THE
FACE OF THE FUTURE?

Take part in our fabulous competition. Simply send in a photograph of yourself and **YOU** might be selected to dress in the latest styles and walk the catwalk in our fantastic

'FACE OF THE FUTURE'

competition to find the next **supermodel**!

Ben sniggered. 'Dream on, sis!' He started to do the kind of silly dance he imagined his sister doing – not that he'd ever seen her dancing, but he had a good imagination and he knew it would wind her up. Carrie ignored him, which wound up Ben instead.

The family cat, Rustbucket, peered into the room for a second and wisely decided not to get involved. She went to find somewhere quiet and peaceful.

'What are you doing?' Sennapod asked him, applying another layer of black eyeliner.

'Dancing.'

'That is dancing? I'd like to do that again. I haven't danced for more than four and a half thousand years. Not since I was covered in bandages and stuffed into that coffin.'

'Were you a good dancer?' asked Ben.

'The Pharaoh was always the best. Everyone said so.'

'Yeah, but that was because if you didn't say the Pharaoh was best, you ended up being thrown to the crocodiles,' Carrie pointed out.

'Of course. We had to feed the crocodiles with something, and they are sacred animals. Nearly all the animals in Ancient Egypt were sacred, especially cats.' He gazed fondly at Crusher of Worms (alias Tiddles), a sleek and elegant black cat with a gold earring in one ear. Crusher of Worms was Sennapod's cat, also brought back to life from thousands of years ago. Both Tiddles and

Rustbucket were very fond of Sennapod. The Pharaoh seemed to have a special way with all cats and often found himself being followed by moggies he'd never seen before.

Carrie jumped up and switched on the radio. 'OK, Senny, show us what you can do. Strut your stuff.'

'Strut my stuff?' repeated the Pharaoh.

'She means, show us a dance,' interpreted Ben.

Sennapod got to his feet and began a slow, stiff series of movements. His arms shot out at strange angles. He raised and lowered his legs at odd moments. Every so often he

would slowly turn himself round while making weird, hen-pecking movements with his head and rolling his eyes.

Ben and Carrie had never seen anything like it. Ben collapsed in hysterics, but Carrie just stared, gob-smacked.

'Senny! That is *so* cool!'

'Cool?' queried the Pharaoh, and Ben laughed.

'Yeah, you know, cool, like hot.'

'Cool is hot?' Now Sennapod was totally confused.

'Hot is the new cool,' Ben declared.

But Carrie grabbed Sennapod and insisted that he show her his weird dance routine again while she followed, step by step. 'My friends are going to love this,' she murmured happily. 'It is just so brilliant.'

Sennapod slowly bent his body into yet another gawky shape. He stopped and frowned. 'If you do not dance like this, how do you dance?'

Carrie grinned and leapt on to her bed, where she began the wildest series of twists and contortions, leaping up, shaking her head and hair, punching the air with her fists and gyrating her hips like every pop star on telly.

The High Lord of All Egypt, the Supreme Pharaoh Sennapod, He Whose Name Shall Rumble Down The Ages, watched with increasing astonishment, while Ben fell about laughing. As far as he was concerned, Carrie was making a fool of herself; but Sennapod was gripped by the performance.

He climbed on to Carrie's bed and began to bounce up and down, faster and faster. A smile crept on to his lips. He started to punch the air. He shook his head so hard his

crown fell off. He swayed his hips. He
wiggled his bottom. Crusher of Worms fled
the room in disgust.

'Fantastic!' Carrie panted, turning
the radio up even louder. 'You're really
good!' The pair of them were now deep
into a copy-cat routine. Carrie showed
Sennapod the moves, and the Pharaoh
copied her.

'I am hot!' he shouted. 'I am the new
cool!'

'Me too,' yelled Carrie.

The door burst open. Mrs Lightspeed
hurried in and switched off the radio. 'Are
you trying to deafen the entire street? Did
you know there's a crack on the ceiling
downstairs where you two have been leaping
up and down? Get off that bed at once, both
of you.'

Carrie duly got down but Sennapod

remained, glaring back at Mrs Lightspeed.
'And you, Senny – get down.'

Sennapod drew himself up to his full
height, planted his hands on his hips and
fixed Mrs Lightspeed with a look of utter
contempt. 'Begone, foul woman!' he roared.
'How dare you interrupt the Royal Dance
of the Pharaoh! You are nothing but a
worm in my presence. I am He Whose
Name Shall –'

'Yes, we know,' interrupted Mrs
Lightspeed. 'But while you are living in my
house, you will behave yourself because I am
the Queen of . . .' She hesitated for a
moment.

'Kwiggly Kwoo?' Ben suggested quietly.

'Kwiggly Kwoo,' said Mrs Lightspeed
with a regal nod of the head.

Sennapod raised his eyebrows with
interest and stepped down from the bed.

'The Queen of Kwiggly Kwoo? Why have you never told me this before?'

'You never asked,' said Mrs Lightspeed evenly. 'Enough of this nonsense. If you want to dance, that's fine by me, but you do not deafen the whole area for miles around and you do not leap about on the beds. Is that understood?'

'I have never heard of Kwiggly Kwoo,' said the Pharaoh. 'Where is it?'

'Over there,' said Mrs Lightspeed, pointing vaguely beyond the bedroom door.

'Do you have many subjects?'

'You do not question a queen,' said Mrs Lightspeed stiffly. 'Now, if you are going to continue dancing, go out into the garden.'

Carrie could no longer bear this nonsense. 'Senny, Mum is not the Qu—'

'I said you do *not* question the Queen of Kwiggly Kwoo!' insisted Mrs Lightspeed,

with a twinkle in her eye. Sennapod hurried
downstairs without looking back, pushing
Carrie in front of him.

As soon as they were safely at the bottom,
Mrs Lightspeed shut the bedroom door and
collapsed on the bed in hysterics.

Underneath her, and getting rather
rumpled and crumpled by her wriggling

weight, was the magazine with the
competition. Not only had Carrie cut out
and filled in the entry form, it was
already in an envelope, in a
post box, waiting
for the postman to
collect it.

FACE OF THE
FUTURE

If Mrs Lightspeed
had known what that
letter was going to lead to, she would not
have found anything funny at all, no matter
whether she was the Queen of Kwiggly
Kwoo or not.

2 Here Comes Trouble

Of course it is highly unusual to find a four-and-a-half-thousand-year-old Ancient Egyptian Pharaoh living with a small family in a small house in a small town in Britain. It had happened in a highly unusual way, beginning with an ill-matched pair of treasure-seeking criminals.

Grimstone had once been the head of the local museum's Ancient Egyptian collection. He was tall and thin, with a large, narrow, sharp-edged nose and chilling eyes. Grimstone was the mastermind and a man who would stop at nothing to get his hands on riches.

And then there was Professor Jelly – short, fat, and willing to do anything as long as he was paid in sweets. The mere thought of a gumdrop made his mouth dribble. Jelly was an Egyptologist and he had worked in the museum with Grimstone, where there were several Ancient Egyptian mummies and also their sacred animals, especially cats.

These two men had discovered that hidden in one mummy case at the museum was a map that held the key to a treasure even more fabulous than that of Tutankhamun. Above everything else that he desired (and he desired an awful lot),

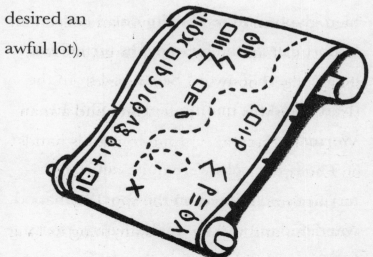

Grimstone wanted to get his hands on that priceless treasure. The mere thought of it made him start drooling.

These two dribbling criminals (because that is what they really were) had opened up the mummy case. Inside they found the mummified body of Sennapod, He Whose Name Shall Rumble Down The Ages, a forgotten Pharaoh from the Four Fifths Dynasty. Jelly had found a manuscript inside the coffin and he translated the hieroglyphs and read them out. Unfortunately the hieroglyphs turned out to be a curse that awoke Sennapod from the dead – and his mummified cat, Crusher of Worms.

The two crooks were quite naturally terrified and fainted on the spot. Sennapod wandered off into the night, feeling pretty bad because he hadn't had anything to eat for four and a half thousand years. (Besides, it was his birthday and nobody had sent him a card.)

Eventually the exhausted Pharaoh had collapsed with hunger outside a Mister Freezee ice-cream van. Luckily for him, the owner of the van, Tony Lightspeed, was the sort of kind person who rescues birds with broken wings and hedgehogs with tyre marks. He took Sennapod home, and the Pharaoh had been living with them ever since.

The two crooks had done everything they could to track down the Pharaoh and get the treasure map. They were pretty sure it was in the Lightspeeds' house, but they had no idea where. Sennapod was the only person who knew that, and he wasn't telling anyone.

Jelly and Grimstone had once tried to

force the secret from Sennapod and had ended up in jail as a result. That would probably have been the end of their wicked schemes to get their beastly mitts on the unspeakably sparkly treasure, had it not been for Grimstone's mother, Seraphina.

Where her son was thin, Seraphina Grimstone bulged. She bulged in every direction. Her body was rammed and crammed into clothes at least two sizes too small. The result was that she looked like a lumpy and inedible sausage on the point of bursting out of its skin.

And where her son was scowly and angry and miserable, Seraphina was bubbly and cheerful and full of smiles. In fact, Seraphina and her son had only one thing in common: they both had evil minds that were constantly dreaming up plans of wickedness and cunning that were beyond belief.

Seraphina knew all about the treasure and, like her son, she had not stopped thinking about how to get her hands on it ever since. Today she was visiting Grimstone and Jelly in jail. It was something she did quite regularly, so that they could discuss plans for (1) The Great Escape, and (2) Getting the Treasure, and (3) Spending It.

Seraphina leant towards them and whispered, hoping that the ever-present guard could not hear their discussion.

'I've brought you some yummy chocolate cake,' she said.

'Has it got a file in it?' demanded Grimstone. 'Then I can file through the bars and escape.'

'Good Lord, no,' chuckled Seraphina.

'But it has got hundreds and thousands
sprinkled on the top.'

'Then I don't want it,' growled
Grimstone.

'My little chicken chops, still the same old
grumpy-pot. Are you sure you don't want
some of Mummy's lovely sponge?'

Professor Jelly licked
his lips and gazed
longingly at the cake.
'Um, I don't mind
eating it,' he said,
and Seraphina
pushed it across
to him.

'Hey, you!' yelled the guard,
Petty Officer Fudd. 'Don't touch that cake
until it's been checked. I know what you
visitors are like, smuggling in duplicate keys
and things. You're just as bad as this lot

behind bars. Pass that cake up here for checking.'

Seraphina smiled cheerfully and pulled the cake away from the drooling professor.

'There we are, Officer,' she bubbled, wiggling her fat fingers at him. 'Why don't you try some yourself? I made it with my own dinky little hands.'

Petty Officer Fudd eyed the cake with enormous suspicion. 'That is exactly what worries me,' he began. 'You may have put something in this cake, perhaps something to put me to sleep, or even something poisonous that would kill me!'

'Good heavens above!' cried Seraphina in mock horror. 'As if I would do such a thing. You prison wardens are such a suspicious bunch. That sponge is my best, my most luscious, delicious chocolate delight.'

By this time Jelly's eyes were almost out on stalks and his tongue was dangling from his mouth like an octopus's tentacle.

'Right,' said Fudd. 'I'll soon have this checked out.' He seized his truncheon, plunged it into the centre of the cake and began stirring it round and round, reducing the cake to a soggy mash. Jelly began to whimper quietly.

'Hmmm. Can't see anything suspicious in here,' announced Fudd. 'You may as well have it back.'

The plate crashed back down in front of Professor Jelly. In front of him now sat what looked like a cow pat that had been sprinkled with hundreds and thousands. (Actually most of the hundreds and thousands had disappeared into the sludgy mixture, so all that was left on top were a few tens and units.)

'You see,' said Seraphina evenly. 'It was a chocolate cake all along. I told you. Look how much you've upset Professor Jelly.'

'Stop snivelling,' hissed Grimstone. 'Once we get out of here we'll find that treasure, and then you can have a whole mountain of chocolate cake.'

'Promise?' sniffed Jelly, but his partner had turned back to Seraphina.

'Just what is your plan, Mum?'

(It may come as a surprise to learn that arch-criminals call their mum 'Mum', but they do, because that is exactly what they are. And they call their dad 'Dad', too.)

'I am still working on it,' said Seraphina, smiling and tapping her nose. 'All I can tell you at this time is that trousers are involved.'

Even as she spoke, Seraphina's eyes were darting round the prison, taking in all the details. She wanted to know where all the doors were and where they led. She wanted to know how many guards were on duty and where they stood. She wanted to know how the prison operated and, most of all, she wanted to know how she was going to spring her son and his fat friend.

Professor Jelly had finally overcome his disgust and was busily dipping one finger into the chocolate accident and popping it into his mouth. It didn't taste too bad after all, at least not when compared with prison food.

Seraphina lowered her voice. 'The next time I come a-visiting, I want you both to be ready. I can't tell you exactly what the plan is, but make sure you are ready to drop everything and make a run for it.'

Grimstone's mouth twisted into a tight smile. 'Escape at last! And then we can hunt down that stupid pompous Pharaoh and all his silly friends. That treasure is as good as ours.'

'That's my boy!' murmured Seraphina, and she gave Grimstone a kiss on the cheek.

'Urgh! Urgh!' he growled, pushing her away and wiping a sleeve across his face.

Seraphina turned to Petty Officer Fudd and laughed. 'He never was a mummy's boy,' she purred. She got to her feet and sidled up to the guard. 'He never did like a kiss and a cuddle. How about you?'

Officer Fudd gave a sudden yelp as something pinched his bottom. 'Gerroff! Leave me alone or I'll call the guard!'

'You *are* the guard,' Seraphina pointed out. 'I love men in uniform. I was only being friendly.'

'Well, you can kindly be friendly with someone else,' said Fudd, hastily unlocking the door so that Seraphina could leave.

'Bye, boys!' she cried as she waved back to them. 'See you next time!' She fluttered her eyelashes at Officer Fudd. 'Bye-bye,' she cooed. 'I'll see you again, too.'

Seraphina made her way home, deep in thought. A plan was taking shape in her wicked mind. Yes, it should work well!

Escaping from the prison was going to be so easy, but first of all she needed to do some shopping. There were some vital things she required to put her plan into action, and top of the list was —

Duplicate keys to the cells? No.

A file for the prison bars? No.

Dynamite, maybe? No.

What Seraphina
needed first of all
was a big bag of
cherries.

3 What a Shower!

Carrie was speechless. This was a big improvement on the normal situation as far as Ben was concerned, but it didn't last long. Carrie raced round the house, showing the letter to everyone, rattling the paper in their faces.

'Calm down, calm down,' said Mrs Lightspeed. 'Show me what it is.'

'It's a letter!' squeaked Carrie.

'Yes. I can see that.'

'It's *the* letter!'

'OK, it's *the* letter, but what does *the* letter say?'

'I've got a test!'

Eve Lightspeed was still in the dark. 'Carrie, you had a test at school last month, a maths test, remember? You weren't at all

32

excited about that, so what's special about this one?'

'It's not that kind of test,' explained Carrie, slowly returning to Planet Earth. 'It's more like an audition. It's that competition for the "Face of the Future". They liked the photo I sent in. They want to see me! Me!'

Ben pointed a finger at her and screwed up his face in horror. 'You've got a test for the supermodel thingy? You? Ugly mug?'

Carrie wrinkled her nose at him. 'Yes, so, you see, this ugly mug obviously isn't as ugly as you think.'

Mrs Lightspeed was reading through the letter. 'I didn't know you'd entered yourself for this.'

'I did tell you, Mum.'

'Was I listening?'

'No, but I did tell you.' Carrie's face fell. 'You don't mind, do you?'

Mrs Lightspeed beamed at her daughter.
'Of course not, Carrie. I think it's
marvellous. You might get on the telly.'

'The nightmare continues,' groaned Ben.

'Don't be horrible,' said Mrs Lightspeed,

and she smiled at Carrie again. 'I'm very proud of you. When is the competition?'

'Tomorrow,' Carrie answered dreamily.

'Tomorrow!' cried Mrs Lightspeed. 'But that's ... that's tomorrow! I mean, it's like yesterday! It's such short notice. You need to get your hair done. You need new clothes, you need – '

'– a new face,' Ben butted in.

'Ha ha ha ha ha.' Carrie gave an icy little laugh and turned to her mother. 'It's OK, Mum, stop fretting. It says here that they will give me clothes to wear when I get there, and they do my make-up and hair and everything.' She was doing little on-the-spot jumps all the time she was speaking. 'I'm so excited I can't stay still.'

'That's all very well for you, Carrie, but in that case I shall need to get my hair done and get a new dress. I don't want those magazine people thinking your mother is some old fishwife. Has your father finished putting in the new shower yet? Trust him to go messing about with important things like showers at a time like this when we all need one.'

Ben went upstairs and poked his head into the bathroom. Tony Lightspeed was finishing off the ceiling with a coat of yellow paint. Sennapod was sitting on the toilet seat with Tiddles at his feet and Rustbucket on his lap, watching him work.

'Wow,' breathed Ben, and his father grinned.

'It is pretty good, isn't it? What do you think of the shower?'

'Cool,' said Ben.

'Hot is the new cool,' declared Sennapod, a remark that left Mr Lightspeed looking a trifle puzzled.

'It doesn't just do hot and cool. It also does all temperatures in between. I think your mother will be very pleased – and Carrie, of course.'

'She's been selected for a modelling competition, Dad,' Ben grumbled. 'If she wins, we'll never hear the end of it. She's always shovelling make-up on her face as it is.'

'A modelling competition? Who would have thought it? Good for her.'

Ben could not understand why both his parents thought it was such a good idea. As far as he was concerned, his sister looked like a horse. However, he changed his mind a bit when Mrs Lightspeed pointed out that at least he would get a day up in London and maybe afterwards they could go to the cinema to watch *Star Wars – Episode 5008: the Sequel to the Prequel's Sequel of the Sequel's Prequel.*

'What is modelling?' asked Sennapod.

Ben yawned very loudly. 'It's incredibly boring, Senny. It's when clothes designers show off their latest fashions that they want people to wear. They put them on young men and women who look good in them and then get old men and women to buy them because they think it will make them look young again.'

'That's a rather cynical view of the world you have,' observed Mr Lightspeed with a little smile.

'Dad, I'm ten.'

'Oh. Right. That explains it, then.'

However, Sennapod was very interested in Ben's explanation and he plucked at Ben's sleeve. 'I could buy these clothes and they will make me look younger?'

'I don't think you'll look younger, but you might feel younger,' said Mr Lightspeed.

'Then I must go, too. I may want to buy some of these new fashions.'

'Yes, well, you certainly look old,' Ben pointed out. 'And you certainly need a make-over.'

'Make-over?' asked Sennapod.

'Yes. It's like what Dad has just been doing to the bathroom. The old bathroom looked old and shabby, just like you do now. But Dad has put in a new shower and new tiles and painted the ceiling, and now the bathroom looks younger and fresher – in other words, it's had a make-over.'

Sennapod nodded and smiled. He felt that this was just what he needed. His four-and-a-half-thousand-year-old bones sometimes creaked a lot, and some new clothes and a new image would make him feel younger and fitter. He got to his feet and made his announcement.

'I shall come too. I need a make-over. Prepare my chariot.'

Mr Lightspeed sighed. 'No chariot, I'm afraid, Senny. You know that. We'll go in Mister Freezee, as usual.'

'I wish you had a BMW, Dad. Tim Bragg's dad has got a BMW.'

Mr Lightspeed smiled at Ben and flung a comforting arm round his shoulder. 'Ben, surely you know, ice-cream vans *are* the new BMWs.'

The following morning was complete chaos, and that was only five minutes after everyone had got up. They all wanted to use the new shower, but Mr Lightspeed insisted that they all come into the bathroom together so he could show them how it worked. It was brand new, after all.

One by one they had to stand in the bath behind the shower curtain while Mr Lightspeed pointed out the different controls.

'Dad, I *have* used a shower before,' sighed Ben.

'Yeah, like last century,' Carrie muttered.

'That's the "ON" button,' said Mr Lightspeed.

'Does that mean it goes on when you press it?' asked Ben.

'Yes, it —' Tony Lightspeed broke off. 'You're winding me up, aren't you?'

'I can read, Dad.'

'OK, OK. Senny, swap places with Ben. Stand in the bath there.'

The Pharaoh climbed into the bath and gazed at the shiny new shower box. It all looked very interesting, and certainly he had never seen anything like it before.

'What does it do?' he asked.

'It washes you,' said Carrie.

'Like handmaidens?' Sennapod often found it difficult to forget his pampered past.

'No, not like handmaidens, like a shower,' sighed Mrs Lightspeed.

'This dial controls the temperature,' explained Mr Lightspeed. 'Turn this way for cold and this way for hot.'

'Hot is the new —'

'Yes, we know. This button switches the water on. Look, it says "ON".'

'This button?'

'Yes.'

'I press it?'

'Yes.'

Thinking this was an instruction, Sennapod pressed it. Surprise, surprise! A hard jet of cold water came swooshing out of the shower-head and struck him full in the face. He staggered back, stumbled against the end of the bath, crashed

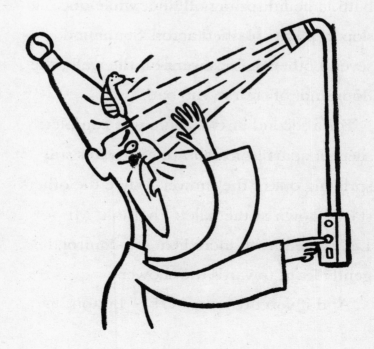

forwards, grabbed at the shower curtain for support, ripped it from its runner and slid sideways into the bath, sending his feet shooting up at the far end, where they slammed into the little shelf above the bath, catapulting into the air the tin of yellow paint that Mr Lightspeed had been using. It spun upwards for a short distance before crashing down on to the inside edge of the bath. The lid sprang off and, while one big slop of paint splashed across Sennapod, several other dollops went on the walls, the floor and, of course, the bath itself.

For a second or two there was complete silence, apart from the noise of water still spraying out of the shower. While the others stared down at the fallen Pharaoh, Mr Lightspeed, with incredible self-control, gently leant towards the shower.

'And if you press the "OFF" button,' he

explained evenly, 'the water is turned off.'

Sennapod struggled to his feet. His crown was crushed. His royal robe (which had once been Mrs Lightspeed's dressing-gown) was covered in yellow paint. His face was thunderous. He pointed a bony finger at the entire family.

'Worms!' he screeched. 'You are but worms beneath the gaze of Osiris!'

'Demoted again,' mumbled Ben. 'Only yesterday he said I was human. Now he's calling me a worm again.'

'You have desecrated the living Pharaoh. You shall be torn apart by crocodiles, trodden on by hippopotamuses, ripped to shreds by vultures and stung by a million hornets.'

'Is that all?' asked Carrie. 'Listen, Senny, this is all your fault. It's no good blaming us. Besides, if we are worms, you really can't

expect anything better. Worms don't know
how to operate showers, so you can't blame
us.'

'Yes, that's true.' There was a murmur of
agreement from the rest of the family. They
huddled closer together and gazed back at
the Royal King of Egypt, waiting to see
what he would do next.

Sennapod's face suddenly crumpled. 'But
I want some new clothes,' he moaned,
fingering his paint-spattered robe. 'How can

I go out in public looking like this?'

'The competition!' squealed Carrie. 'We've got to get to the competition! I've got to be the Face of the Future. What do I do? What do I do?'

4 Cherry Surprise

When Seraphina Grimstone returned for some more prison visiting she did not take a chocolate cake with her this time. Instead, she had the most wonderful Black Cherry Bombe. (Note: The dessert was a bombe, not a bomb. A bomb goes BANG! It makes a lot of mess and can't be eaten. However, a bombe goes YUMMY! and everyone likes scoffing one.)

The outside of the bombe was made of meringue and it was almost completely covered with raspberries and morello cherries, which in turn were sprinkled with shavings of dark chocolate. The inside of the bombe was made of cream, mixed with brandy and then frozen, so that it was like ice cream.

Seraphina put it on a large silver dish, covered it with a silver lid, and marched into the Visitors' Room, bearing the platter in front of her as if she was a waitress at the poshest hotel in the world, and not delivering it to some grimy little prison. She beamed across at Grimstone and Jelly.

'Hello, boys! Mummy's here!'

'Is that for us?' asked Professor Jelly, with tears of joy in his eyes.

'Indeed it is, my jolly pair, sort of.'

'I don't like sweet puddings,' scowled Grimstone.

'I know, dear. You never did. In fact I don't think you have ever liked anything. Do you remember your first smile? Of course you don't. You only ever smiled once, when your hamster died. Never mind. Listen up, my pair of cheery chickens, are you ready to rock and roll?'

'Rock and roll?' repeated Grimstone.

'Shake a leg?' Seraphina said suggestively.

'Shake a leg?'

'Wink wink, know what I mean?'
Seraphina added through gritted teeth.

'Oh! You mean you've got an escape plan!' Grimstone cried.

'Sssssh! Try not to tell everyone!' Seraphina lowered her voice. 'In a moment I am going to offer you this dessert ...'

'Oh, goody goody goody!' moaned Professor Jelly.

'... but I'm afraid you can't eat it,' Seraphina finished.

Jelly slumped forwards in despair and began to bang his head on the little table, over and over again. Bump! Bump! Bump! Bump! He moaned gently with each bump.

'No cake. No cake. NO CAKE!'

'When I offer it to you, the guard should come over to investigate, like he did last time. I want you boys to be ready for action. Is that clear?'

Grimstone nodded. Jelly was still busily banging his head on the table. Grimstone grabbed his companion by the scruff of the neck and lifted up the professor's head. 'Do you understand?' he hissed.

'I want to die,' groaned Jelly.

'No you don't. You want to escape, and then you can have as much dessert as you like, all right?'

Professor Jelly straightened up. 'Really?'

'Yes, but first we have to get out. Are you ready for action?'

Professor Jelly nodded and Seraphina pushed the Black Cherry Bombe across the table with as much noise as possible. 'I made this especially for you two boys,' she said loudly.

Petty Officer Fudd spun round at once. 'Oi! You over there! I told you last time, no cakes for the prisoners.'

'But, Officer,' protested Seraphina, fluttering her eyelashes, 'this is simply a Black Cherry Bombe, made with raspberries and cherries and chocolate.'

'Huh! You can dress it up however you want, madam, but you might have put a file in there, or a stick of dynamite, or –'

'I know, you gorgeous man, you said the same thing last time, but I promise you there's nothing inside except brandy and cream.'

Petty Officer Fudd was already getting out his truncheon. 'In that case, madam, you won't mind if I do this, will you?' He plunged his truncheon into the centre of the dessert and began to stir wildly.

Now, to be fair, Seraphina had warned Fudd. She had told him what was inside. It was full of brandy and cream. It was meant to be frozen brandy and cream, of course. But Seraphina had carried it for a long time and, just as she had planned, the cream and brandy were now very unfrozen.

When Fudd smashed his truncheon through the crisp outer walls of meringue, it was just as if he had smashed through the walls of a dam. Brandy and cream came spurting out in an explosion of white froth, soaking Fudd from the chest down.

'Oh no!' he cried, stepping

back and gazing down at his soaked uniform. A strong smell of brandy wafted across the air. Fudd lifted his nose and sniffed. 'The Chief mustn't see me like this. He'll think I've been drinking on duty. Look at the mess!'

Seraphina was on her feet, whipping out a large handkerchief and mopping down the unfortunate prison officer. 'Oh dear, oh dear, indeed you are in a mess, but panic not, my little flower, we shall soon have you spick and span. Here, let me help.' She dabbed away at Fudd's uniform until she had managed to smear the cream over every bit of it.

'Oh my, it seems to be getting worse,' she said. 'Let's get that jacket off you, and you'll have to take your trousers off, too.'

'I can't take my trousers off!' Fudd protested.

'Don't be silly, I'm a nurse,' lied Seraphina. 'You certainly can't let the Chief see you wearing them. Come on, take them off, there's a good boy.'

As the jacket and trousers came off, Seraphina threw them across to Grimstone, who immediately began putting them on, cream or no cream. Petty Officer Fudd was in such a state he didn't even notice. He was moaning and groaning and wondering what to do next.

'I have just the thing to stop you fussing,' said Seraphina cheerfully.

'What's that?' moaned Fudd miserably.

Seraphina plunged a hand into her bag and whipped out a roll of tape. 'Ta-ra! We put one strip across your mouth – it's no use struggling, I have a black belt in Tie-U-Up, the ancient art of nobbling people. And a long strip round your wrists and another

round your ankles and, oh look! We have a
Christmas turkey! Come on, boys, it's time
to go!'

Grimstone, who now looked like one of
the guards, seized Jelly by the scruff of the
neck yet again (he was secretly getting
pleasure out of that bit) and, with his
mother behind him, he marched out of the
Visitors' Room and off down the
path to the entrance to the
jail.

At the gate they
were stopped by
another guard,
who demanded
to know what
they were up to.
Grimstone pushed
Professor Jelly
forwards.

'This fat little rat has spilled cream all over my uniform,' declared Grimstone. 'We are off to the dry cleaners so that he can pay for it.'

'And I'm going with them,' said Seraphina, smiling.

'What a disgusting thing to do,' bellowed the guard at the gate. 'Fancy doing that to an officer's uniform. Go on then, and hurry it up!'

The gate was opened and the three arch-criminals walked clear. Down the road they went, walking steadily until they reached the corner. They turned the corner. They looked at each other, smiled, and in chorus they yelled, 'Run for it!'

5 Walk Like an Egyptian

The Lightspeed household was in chaos as everyone struggled to get changed in time to make it to the 'Face of the Future' competition. Mr Lightspeed got in the way of Carrie. Carrie got in the way of Sennapod. He got in the way of Ben and, to make matters worse, the cats got in the way of everybody.

'I've nothing to wear!' wailed the Pharaoh. 'Why am I cursed with a house like this? I should be in a palace, with a thousand servants. Where is my robe of silk? Where is my tunic of fine sea-cotton? Where are my golden sandals?'

'Try these!' Mr Lightspeed answered, chucking across a pair of his own trousers and a check shirt.

There were a few moments of silence as Sennapod struggled into clothes that he was unused to wearing. At length he appeared in the Lightspeeds' bedroom and demanded to know if he looked royal enough.

The Lightspeeds looked at him. They looked at each other. Then they shook their heads and said, 'No,' in unison.

'You look silly,' added Mrs Lightspeed for good measure. 'Those trousers are for a short, fat person.'

'Thank you,' murmured her husband. 'You're so kind.'

'And you are a tall, thin person and you look silly. You'll just have to wear your bandages, Senny. They're in your chest of drawers. They've been washed.'

Sennapod had hardly ever worn his bandages since he had been rescued by the Lightspeeds. Mrs Lightspeed had made him the special robe. The children had made his crown, and he was very proud of both of them, but the crown was crushed and the robe spattered with paint.

He hurried off to fetch the bandages.

They were the same ones he had worn inside his coffin. He was quite used to wearing them, but not at all used to putting them on. Swathing yourself in bandages is much more difficult than getting someone else to do it for you. Sennapod stood on the landing and tried. He tried and tried.

At his first attempt he tied himself to the stair post. With his second try he bandaged both legs together so that he couldn't move. At the third go he bent down to do his feet and managed to loop bandages round his

feet and his head at the same time, leaving him doubled over. For his fourth attempt he simply cried, 'Help!' Ben had to sort him out.

Finally everyone was ready, and off they went.

Carrie was agog with excitement. Her head was exploding with dreams of stardom, of fame and fortune. She could just picture herself hobnobbing with film stars and pop idols. Her face would be on the front of beauty magazines. She would wear designer clothes every single day. It was going to be brilliant!

They arrived outside the hall where the competition was taking place. Carrie gulped. Her face turned white. There were girls like her everywhere, dozens of them! They were all there for the competition. Carrie froze.

Mr Lightspeed slipped an arm round her

shoulders. 'Ignore them, Carrie. They haven't got what it takes. You go in there and wow those judges. Just be yourself.'

'Yeah,' nodded Ben. 'Be yourself, sis. Argue them to death.'

'Leave her be, Ben,' said Mrs Lightspeed soothingly. 'I don't suppose you'd be brave enough to do what Carrie is doing.'

This was very true, and Ben kept his thoughts to himself after that. However, they were now at the reception desk and the girl behind the counter was looking at Carrie's entry form.

'Oh yes, number one hundred and thirty-seven – you're to go to make-up and then to the dressing-room. Next!' The girl looked up at Sennapod and stared. Her mouth dropped open. Her gaze shifted from Sennapod's made-up head right down to his bandaged toes.

'Oh wow,' she breathed. 'That outfit is just mind-blowing. I love your eyeliner! You are so cool.'

'Hot is the new cool,' Sennapod said stiffly.

'I know, I know, and you are hot! And so cool! Have you got your entry form?'

Mr Lightspeed pushed forwards. 'It's OK, he's with us. He's not taking part.'

'But he *must*,' the girl insisted. 'I mean, he is *it*.'

'I am not an it,' declared the Pharaoh. 'I am He Whose Name Shall Rumble Down The Ages, Lord of Hippos, Master of Worms and All Creeping Things.'

The girl behind the desk was giggling. 'Wow!' she bubbled. 'You are something!'

'I thought you said I was it,' Sennapod pointed out. 'How can I be it if I'm something?'

The girl wasn't listening. She had called over a woman dressed in extraordinary clothes. Her hair was dyed red, orange, green, black and purple. It had been back-combed until it seemed her scalp was exploding. She had a thin beak of a nose and a scarlet gash for a mouth. The girl introduced her.

'This is Tamara Salata.'

Carrie almost died on the spot. 'Tamara Salata?' she squeaked. 'The top fashion designer?'

'Darling, you're so kind. Yes, I am the top fashion designer and also one of the judges, one of the most important judges – no, the most important judge.' Tamara studied Sennapod from top to toe. 'You are the most exotic, gorgeous human being I have ever seen. You are a work of art, monsieur. Your sense of fashion is sublime, exquisite. Your clothes are simply not of this world.'

'Too right,' muttered Ben. 'They're bandages from an Ancient Egyptian coffin, you daft bat!'

'Ssssh!' hissed Mrs Lightspeed, but it didn't matter because Tamara was far too busy admiring Sennapod anyway. She insisted that he go with her.

'Darling, we must get you into make-up.'

The Pharaoh perked up. He liked make-up.

'The handmaidens will see to your face and so on.' Tamara leant towards Sennapod and whispered in his ear, 'I always call them handmaidens. The whole business of fashion is just so, so decadent, don't you think? Then it will be straight on to the catwalk. Darling, you are going to be a star!'

And before the Lightspeeds could register what was happening, both Carrie and Sennapod had been whisked away to be prepared for the 'Face of the Future'. All they could do was file into the huge hall and take their seats, along with the rest of the audience and the press men and the cameramen and the TV crews.

The lights went down. The spots came on. A thunderous, pounding wave of music crashed from a hundred speakers and the show began. One after another the would-be models came tripping down the catwalk, wearing incredible costumes that looked as if they had come from outer space.

'Where would you wear something like that?' Mrs Lightspeed kept asking.

'I wouldn't,' said Mr Lightspeed. 'It's for ladies. Shall I buy you one?'

And then Carrie appeared, along with Sennapod. Carrie had been stuck inside what looked like a pair of jeans and a matching denim jacket, except she was also wearing a ballet dancer's pink tutu round her waist and a miniature version of the same thing on each wrist. As for Sennapod, he hadn't changed at all. He was trailing his bandages and walking along as if he'd just escaped from some horror film. However, his face was a bit different, because he had been thoroughly made up and his face was now in full, glorious colour.

As they reached the catwalk the music suddenly changed and the two of them began to dance. It was not the kind of dance that anyone in the audience had seen before, apart from Ben. It was the dance that Sennapod had taught Carrie only a few days earlier.

They came up the catwalk, bit by bit, slowly twisting their bodies into weird angular shapes, making their heads do that curious pecking movement, and it was mesmerizing. The audience went wild. They began to clap. They cheered. They got to their feet and stamped and whooped and yelled themselves silly.

This was it! This was something! This was the new hot, cold and lukewarm all at once! Amazing! That costume the man had on

was breathtaking: so simple, so stark, so ...
bandagey! Flashbulbs popped. Video cams
whirred. Microphones were thrust towards
the catwalk.

Tamara Salata flounced on to the stage

and began curtseying and bowing and
blowing kisses in every direction.

'Everyone thinks she created Senny's
costume,' muttered Mrs Lightspeed. 'It's
only his old bandages. I had to wash those
filthy things.'

She tried to shout out and tell everyone,
but the roar of the crowd drowned her.
Sennapod was a knockout. He was whisked
away to be photographed and interviewed
and asked billions of questions, while the
Lightspeeds stayed in their seats, feeling
more and more fed up, especially Carrie.

'I don't believe it. Senny's won
the competition,' she said.
'How did that happen? He's
not a girl. He didn't even
enter. They wanted a girl and
they've chosen him. He's not
even handsome. He's four and

a half thousand years old! It's not fair! It really isn't!'

And Carrie was right. It wasn't fair, but at least it hadn't been Sennapod's fault. He didn't really have any idea what was going on. He was delighted with the handmaidens. He was overwhelmed by the roar of the crowd. It was just like the ancient days, so long ago. The people had liked his dance, and quite right too. It was the Royal Dance of the Pharaoh and they had to like it. If they didn't, he'd throw them to the crocodiles. All Sennapod needed now was his palace and his bath of asses' milk, and it would be just like being back in Ancient Egypt. Little did he know that the palace might be arriving sooner than he thought.

6 Plan Number One

Seraphina settled down in front of the
television and put her tired feet up on a
coffee table. She smiled happily. Her son,
Grimstone, was back home at last, along
with his friend Jelly. They had eaten a lovely
supper, and now they wanted to watch the
news on telly, because they thought there
might be an interesting item all about them.

The newscaster, Tamsin Plank, stared
seriously at the camera. 'News today of a
breakout from a top security prison. The
criminals, Grimstone and Jelly, managed to
escape with the help of a prison visitor. One
of the guards was knocked out and left for
dead.'

'We were too soft on him,' snarled
Grimstone.

'Sssh. There's more,' hissed Seraphina.

'In some kind of bizarre ritual the guard was smeared with chocolate, cream and morello cherries. It's thought the criminals had planned to turn Petty Officer Fudd into a giant cake that they could sell to the public for a large sum of money. That way the only

witness to their crime would have been eaten. Luckily, they were disturbed before they could carry out their plan. Police are now hunting the two men and one woman.'

'Turn the guard into a cake?' muttered Seraphina. 'I wish we'd thought of that. Oh, look!' she suddenly squeaked. 'It's them! It's them!'

The next item was on. 'We report now from the competition to find the "Face of the Future". Hundreds of hopeful girls turned up to audition but were completely upstaged by a man claiming to be an Ancient Egyptian Pharaoh. His costume and dance routine drew wild applause from the audience. It is thought that the man, who says he is four and a half thousand years old, has been signed up by fashion diva Tamara Salata. His highly individual dress sense, a stunning combination of bandages and exotic make-up, coupled with his eerie dancing, looks set to break the fashion moulds and start a whole new trend. This is Tamsin Plank signing off for today and I'm going straight out to get myself some bandages.'

Seraphina watched the performance with delight. 'Oh my,' she chortled. 'Aren't they idiots? Fancy thinking those bandages are the new fashion. They must all be mad. But, my dears, I think I have a cunning little idea.'

'So do I,' growled Grimstone. 'We go to their house and seize the map. Then we go and find the treasure and then we go and spend loads of money. I shall buy a house as big as a castle, with battlements and everything –'

'That *is* a castle, dear boy,' said Seraphina.

'Good. I shall buy a castle and a yacht and a personal jet and a helicopter and a sports car.'

'And I shall buy a chocolate factory,' sighed Professor Jelly.

'All right, boys, enough dreaming. There are two problems with your little plan. You seem to forget that the Lightspeeds will recognize you straight away. Secondly, you are on the run from prison. The police are after you. As soon as you show your faces you'll be arrested. But my face is not nearly so well known. I have a much better idea.'

So it was that next day the doorbell rang at 27 Templeton Drive and, when Ben opened it, a large lady, wearing an enormous hat and a great wodge of scarf draped round her shoulders, asked if she could speak to Sennapod. Ben invited her in and Seraphina

Grimstone soon found
herself sitting in the
Lightspeeds' front
room.

She could not help wondering if the
treasure map was somewhere near by.
Under the clock on the mantelpiece maybe?
Stuffed between the books on the shelf?
Tucked behind one of the pictures on the
wall?

'Charming house, absolutely delightful,' she burbled.

'You should see the bathroom,' hinted Ben.

'Oh?'

'It's a mess,' said Carrie. 'Dad's redecorating, again.'

Seraphina nodded, although she had no idea what they were on about and she didn't want to know about the bathroom anyhow. At this moment Crusher of Worms stalked into the room, tail held high.

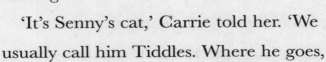

'What a beautiful cat!' cried Seraphina. 'So elegant. I love that earring.'

'It's Senny's cat,' Carrie told her. 'We usually call him Tiddles. Where he goes,

Senny follows, and vice versa. They're inseparable.'

Sure enough, the cat was closely followed by the Pharaoh himself. Seraphina immediately got to her feet. She knelt before him, murmuring, 'Your Majesty, O Your Majesty, Osiris on Earth, Mighty Hunter, etc., etc.,' and generally carrying on in a thoroughly fawning manner.

Sennapod was overwhelmed. He drew himself up and said: 'You may kiss my feet.'

'Thank you,' said Seraphina. She gritted her teeth and did as commanded.

'You may rise and speak.'

Ben and Carrie were sniggering quietly in the corner. They would never let Senny get away with anything like this, but this daft lady seemed quite happy to do just as he said.

Seraphina got to her feet, which took

rather a long time because of her shape and size, but eventually she made it.

She smiled at the Pharaoh and began, 'Great Lord, I come because I have seen your truly majestic performance. I understand that people think you are the "Face of the Future" and that you will set the fashion for years to come.'

'But of course,' answered Sennapod evenly. 'The Pharaoh always leads his people.'

'Yes, I know, but I have heard whispers, O Great One.'

'Whispers?'

'The people plot against you.'

If this was news to the Pharaoh, it was also news to Ben and Carrie. Tiddles leapt

lightly into Sennapod's arms and he held the cat tightly.

'I have heard that Tamara Salata, the fashion diva, intends to make you the most famous face of fashion ever known.'

'That is true. Why should that worry me?'

Seraphina took a step closer and put on her most concerned face. 'Has she told you what she is going to pay you?'

Sennapod's eyes snapped on to Seraphina's. They seemed to glare and glow as he realized that perhaps there was something going on that he should know about.

Seraphina held the Pharaoh's gaze. It was something she was very good at. She could outstare a rattlesnake.

'Are you saying I should be paid?'
Sennapod said slowly.

Seraphina smiled and relaxed a little. She
knew she had him hooked on her bait.
People always wanted money. No matter
how much they had, they always wanted
more, even if they were
the Pharaoh of the
whole of Egypt.

'Paid in
gold,' she
hinted. 'The
fashion diva is
going to make a lot of
money out of you. She
is already marketing
your costume of
bandages as a design
of her own.'

'She shall be

cursed!' roared Sennapod. 'I shall send a plague of fleas to infest her body. I shall have her eyes pecked out by ravens. I shall plunge her feet into cold porridge.'

This last torture seemed a trifle strange to Seraphina. 'Porridge?' she repeated.

'He doesn't like porridge,' Carrie told her.

The Pharaoh turned his gaze back on Seraphina. 'So, woman, why do you come here, kissing my feet and telling me this?'

Seraphina sighed. At last they had come to the point. 'O Mighty Pharaoh, the Living Osiris, He Whose Name Shall Crumble on the Pages –'

'Rumble Down The Ages,' Sennapod corrected her.

'Yes. I have come because I can work for you. I can protect you from the fashion diva Tamara Salata. I can make sure you get what you want.'

Sennapod's ears pricked up. He could get what he wanted! 'Hmmmm. I see. Does that mean *anything*?'

'Anything, Emperor of Hippos and Tickler of Little Frogs.'

'The diva Tamara gave me handmaidens.'

'You shall have as many handmaidens as you wish.'

'And asses' milk for my bath.'

'I have a big ass,' answered Seraphina evenly, thinking of Professor Jelly.

'I shall need a palace ...'

'Consider it done,' fawned Seraphina.

Sennapod closed his eyes and gave a little nod. This was much more like it. Here was a woman who understood his true worth, a woman who recognized what it meant to be the Living God, the Pharaoh, the Ruler of Upper and Lower Egypt. 'Then we shall leave at once,' he said.

'Senny!' cried Ben. 'You can't just go!'

Seraphina sensed that Ben and Carrie could ruin her plans. Maybe she could offer them a little bribe. 'Perhaps you would like something for your friends?' she suggested, but Sennapod shook his head.

'They are worms,' he said dismissively.

'Thanks a bundle, Senny! After all we've done for you.'

The Pharaoh looked surprised at this attack. 'I am the Pharaoh. You had no choice. Everyone has to help me, or they get –'

'– thrown to the crocodiles,' snapped Carrie. 'OK, you go then, you selfish prig. I hate you. You've ruined my competition and now you repay what we've done for you by ignoring us and calling us worms. Go on, go with fat-face here, and I hope you rot!'

And with that Seraphina and the Pharaoh

were practically
pushed out
through the
front door by
Carrie, and she
slammed it after
them. She glared
furiously at the

shut door for a few moments and then sank
to the floor, crying her eyes out.

7 A Bit of a Mistake

Ben stared at the closed door. He could not believe that Sennapod had walked out on them like that. 'I mean, just because that woman promised him a palace and handmaidens and asses' milk! Anyhow, I don't know why you're blubbing, Carrie.'

A giant sniff came from the crumpled heap on the floor. Carrie raised her head. 'I am not blubbing. I'm upset, that's all, and so is Crusher of Worms. Look, he's scratching at the door. He wants Senny back.'

In fact Crusher of Worms was getting rather frantic. He leapt up at the front door. He scratched it so hard that his claws left deep grooves down the wood. At length he began hurling himself at the door as if trying to break through it. Ben watched all this

with a growing sense that something was
wrong.

'I think Tiddles is trying to tell us
something.'

'Yeah, like he wants to go out?' (Sniff).
'Do you want a tiddle, Tiddles?'

'Something's up. You know how sensitive
that cat is. He always knows when
something is going wrong.'

Ben considered the cat for a few
seconds more then came to a
decision. He reached
down, grabbed
Carrie by the arm
and hauled her to
her feet.

'Come on,
we're going
after him.'

'What? That slimy creep? You've got to be joking.'

Ben had opened the front door and he watched as Tiddles shot out and began trotting quickly up the road. Ben pulled his sister out after the cat. 'We're going to follow Tiddles. He's sure to lead us to Senny. I reckon there's something fishy going on. There's something about that woman that I don't like, something about her eyes that reminded me of someone, but I can't think who. I just know she's bad news.'

Carrie hurried along beside her brother rather reluctantly. 'Do we have to do this?'

'No, you can go home if you want. But I think Senny's walking into big trouble, and he's going to need our help.'

'Serves him right,' panted Carrie.

'Maybe, but you know as well as I do that he's just a bit big-headed really. He hasn't got a clue what's going on. People take advantage of him. He could be getting into

really serious danger. Can't you run any faster? We're losing Tiddles. Look! There they are, up ahead, Senny and that woman.'

Sennapod and Seraphina were marching along the street, some way in front, deep in conversation, with Sennapod's bandages flapping behind him as he strode along. He cut quite a figure.

'Where will my palace be?' asked the Pharaoh. 'It will be made of marble, of course, from the Upper Nile?'

'Most certainly, Your Hugely High Highness, the Upper Nile,' simpered Seraphina, a cheerful smile completely masking her evil thoughts. Behind that smile she was thinking: this man is a fool! Soon I shall get him home and he will be completely in my power and we shall have that treasure map off him in no time at all!

As for Sennapod, he was just loving it.

Someone was treating him like royalty at last – not like that scruffy family and that girl who kept complaining every time he pinched her eyeliner. No, this was the real thing. This woman was obviously someone who was going to treat him properly, with all the pomp and splendour that he deserved.

'And I shall need sixteen bathrooms,' Sennapod declared.

'Of course. Everyone should have sixteen bathrooms.'

'Only the Pharaoh has sixteen bathrooms,' Sennapod corrected her. 'The rest can make do with buckets.'

'That's fine,' nodded Seraphina. 'Buckets for the rest of the world. Come on, not far to go now.'

Seraphina cast a backward glance. The hairs on the back of her neck were prickling and she had the distinct feeling that they were being followed. She failed to notice Crusher of Worms, trotting along quite happily almost at Senny's feet. She also failed to see Ben and Carrie suddenly dart out of sight for fear of being spotted.

However, she did notice the ambulance. It had been following them now for some minutes, keeping pace with Seraphina's walking speed. The lights were not flashing. The siren was silent. But it was clear that the ambulance was trailing them. A face at the passenger window was staring out at her. What on earth were they up to?

The ambulance put on a little spurt so that it was now cruising right beside Sennapod and Seraphina. The passenger window slid down and a paramedic called to them.

'Where are you two off to, then?'

'Mind your own business,' snapped Seraphina.

'This *is* our business,' insisted the paramedic. 'That's one of our hospital patients there. He shouldn't be out on the streets in that condition."

Seraphina relaxed and smiled. It was just a stupid mistake, caused by all the bandages. It could easily be explained. 'No, no, he's not a patient,' she corrected. 'He's an Ancient Egyptian Pharaoh from the Four Fifths Dynasty.'

'Really? And I'm the King of China. Come on, let's get him into the ambulance and we'll take him back to hospital.'

Seraphina stopped, and so did the ambulance. She scowled at the paramedic. 'I am telling you he is not one your patients. He's a Pharaoh!'

'In that case you won't mind if we ask him who he is,' said the paramedic. The ambulance doors opened and out stepped two of them. 'Would you mind telling us your name, sir?'

Sennapod was not going to utter his real name. That was sacred. 'My name is He Whose Name Shall Rumble Down The Ages,' he declared.

'Nobody has a stupid name like that,' said the other paramedic. 'I think you had better get into the back of the ambulance quietly or I shall have to inject you with a tranquillizer.'

'You can't do this!' cried Seraphina, stepping between Sennapod and the paramedics. 'This man is the "Face of the Future".'

'Really? Well, I don't like the look of his face at all. He's wearing eyeliner and rouge.'

'All the Ancient Egyptians wore eyeliner and rouge!' Seraphina yelled. 'Didn't they teach you anything at school?'

'Listen, lady, are you going to let us take this patient back to the hospital or not?'

'Definitely not!' bellowed Seraphina, and she began struggling with the paramedics. Sennapod flung out both arms and roared, 'Begone, foul pests! How dare you manhandle my true servant? I shall crush you beneath my feet like small beetles.'

The paramedics glanced at each other and nodded as one. 'He's definitely gone mad. Right, you, into the ambulance.' And, without further ado, Sennapod was bundled unceremoniously into the ambulance and away it went, siren wailing.

That left Seraphina standing by the side of the road, stamping her feet and bellowing after the rapidly disappearing vehicle, 'You stupid fools! I'd almost got him home. The treasure was almost in my grasp. I'll find you!' she screeched. 'I'll find you, wherever you are!' She searched through her handbag, grabbed her mobile and quickly dialled home.

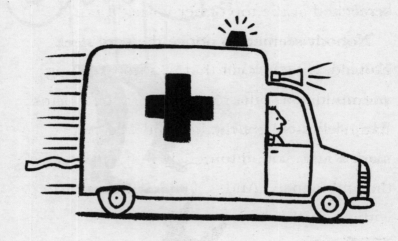

'The idiot's gone and got himself kidnapped by paramedics!' she yelled down the phone to an astonished Grimstone. 'They must have taken him to the local hospital. I'm going get a taxi there now and get him back. Once I've explained everything properly, they'll understand. You two see if you can do something useful until I get back, right?'

Seraphina shoved the phone back in her bag, waved one fat arm high in the air and screeched at the top of her voice, 'Taxi!'

Nobody seemed to notice the very sleek and elegant black cat that was now trotting purposefully up the road. Crusher of Worms had no idea where the hospital was, but somehow he could sense where his master

was, and he was going to make sure that they were reunited.

This whole drama had also been watched by Carrie and Ben. They had taken care not to get themselves involved. They wanted to see what would happen, and they were as surprised as Seraphina was when Sennapod was stuffed into the ambulance and removed.

'Where do you think they'll take him?' pondered Ben.

Carrie put a finger to her chin and gave a theatrical frown. 'Now I wonder where ambulances usually go?'

'All right, stupid question,' admitted Ben. 'We'd better get back and tell Mum and Dad.' So they turned and headed back to the house.

*

Mrs and Mrs Lightspeed were very concerned to learn what had been going on. 'I can't believe such a thing could happen,' complained Mrs Lightspeed. 'Why on earth did they think he was a hospital patient?'

'Mum, he was covered from head to toe in designer bandages,' explained Carrie. 'Ever since that "Face of the Future" competition Sennapod's worn nothing else. Then he went around, cursing the ambulance men in his usual friendly way. Not only did he look like an escaped patient, he acted like a madman.'

'Why didn't you stop them?' asked Mr Lightspeed.

Ben and Carrie glanced at each other. Neither of them felt they were on very safe ground. They had no evidence to prove that something odd was going on, only their gut feelings.

'The woman who came and spoke to Senny – she was weird,' said Ben.

'Darling, Sennapod's weird,' said Eve Lightspeed, smiling.

'I know. But she was promising him a palace and handmaidens and everything. He believed her, but I didn't. I mean, nobody can go round promising palaces and handmaidens, can they?'

Mr Lightspeed shook his head. 'That's true, and it does make things seem a bit fishy. I'm afraid there's more bad news, too. Your mum and I were just watching the news on telly. Grimstone and Jelly have escaped.'

'What?' chorused the children in dismay.

'Exactly. I think we had better try and find Sennapod fast, before he gets himself into serious trouble. He's obviously been taken to the nearest hospital, so it shouldn't be difficult to track him down. But I reckon those two criminals will be after him, too. Come on, into the ice-cream van. It's time we went and played Hunt the Pharaoh.'

8 Hospitalized!

Grimstone put down the telephone and began to pace the room. Professor Jelly watched and waited. Grimstone had a scowling, thoughtful look on his face and Jelly knew it was a bad time to disturb him.

'Do something useful, that's what Mummy said,' muttered Grimstone. 'Do something useful. Something useful that we can do. Go to the hospital? No! We'd be recognized. Find the map? Hmmmm. Now there's a good idea. There's only two possible places it can be – Sennapod has it with him, or he has hidden it at the house of those pesky children.'

Professor Jelly decided to risk a small suggestion. 'Why don't we go and burgle the house?'

'Because the moment we go out of here we shall be recognized and arrested!' snapped Grimstone.

'We could disguise ourselves,' Jelly said.

'And suppose the family is in the house when we want to burgle it?' snapped Grimstone.

'Suppose they're out?' Jelly snapped back. He was beginning to get fed up with Grimstone bossing him around. He thought his ideas were pretty clever.

'Fine. All right. We go and burgle the house. So what are we going to dress up as? Donald Duck and Superman? Or how about this for an idea: we dress up as burglars!'

Professor Jelly ignored Grimstone's sarcasm and instead waddled off to the kitchen.

When he came back he was carrying

several rolls of thin, white gauze. He put them on the table and gave his partner-in-crime a moody glance. 'Designer bandages. We could go out wearing the latest fashion. Nobody will know who we are under all this lot.'

Grimstone actually smiled. His face almost broke in pieces as he did so because it just wasn't used to smiling.

'That is a brilliant idea, Jelly. I always thought you were an idiot, but I have to admit, you do have a brain after all.'

'I'm a professor,' sighed Jelly. 'You don't become a professor without doing a lot of learning.'

'Yes, all right, smarty-pants, now stop wasting time and hand me one of those rolls. I'll do you and then you can do me.'

It took the two men almost an hour to wind the bandages round each other. It was much more difficult than it looked. At one point Jelly had an entire table lamp bandaged to his back, while Grimstone was so well swaddled he couldn't see or breathe. He collapsed on the floor, wriggling and writhing and giving feeble, muffled coughs.

Thinking his friend was having a heart attack, Jelly leapt on top of him and began thumping his chest with his fist. 'One, two, three, four,' he counted, before rolling Grimstone across the floor. 'Into recovery position, then what? Pump arm up and down. No, that doesn't do anything. Oh dear. Lift legs? No. What comes next? Yes, I know! Mouth-to-mouth.'

Professor Jelly scrabbled at the bandages across Grimstone's mouth and started to give mouth-to-mouth resuscitation.

'Splurrgh! Splurrgh!' choked Grimstone, frantically waving his arms around and trying to push the heavy professor off his chest. 'Gerroff! What do you think you're doing?'

'Saving your life,' Jelly said angrily.

'A likely story. Help me up and bandage my head again – properly this time, so that I can see and breathe, if you don't mind.'

Finally they were ready, and they slipped gingerly out through the back door. They collected their bicycles from the shed and set off for the Lightspeeds' house. All the way they kept a sharp lookout for anyone who might spot who they really were, but they needn't have bothered. They were not the only ones covered in bandages. On the way to the house they saw at least seven other people sporting the new look. It seemed as if Sennapod's fashion statement was already catching on.

When they reached the house, they knocked boldly on the front door and promptly ran round the corner and hid.

Nobody answered – because, of course, nobody was in. They slipped round to the back of the house. Grimstone broke a rear window and climbed inside. He unlocked the kitchen door and let the professor in. Then they began to search the house.

They pulled out drawers and tipped their contents on the floor. They opened wardrobes and pulled out all the clothes. They swept everything off the shelves on to the floor, too. Wherever they went, they left a chaotic trail of mess behind them. The more they searched, the crosser they became.

'That map must be here somewhere!' growled Grimstone. 'I can almost smell it! Come on, Jelly, think where it could be. If you were going to hide a priceless treasure map, where would you put it?'

'I'd put it somewhere nobody would look,' Jelly answered truthfully.

'Fool! That doesn't get us anywhere! I've had it. I give up.' Grimstone flung himself down in an armchair amid the jumble of papers and books and clothes. Then just as suddenly he jumped to his feet again.

'OK, I know what to do. We'll go to the hospital.'

'But we shall be recognized.'

'Don't be daft. We're in disguise. Nobody recognized us on the way here. We go to the hospital, find that sneaky son of a snake, Sennapod, and make him give us the map.'

'I'm not sure about this . . .' began Jelly.

'Do you want to be rich beyond your wildest dreams?'

'Of course.'

'Let's go then.'

The two men got back on their bikes, and this time they set off for the hospital.

It just so happened that Petty Officer Fudd was out doing a bit of shopping. He was looking for a new uniform, and while he was out and about he saw the two men cycling up the street. They didn't notice him, but he noticed them. They were very noticeable. If you saw two people wearing bandages from head to toe and riding bikes, you would probably stare too, and this is what Fudd did.

He was not sure that he recognized them, but there was something about that huge, sharp nose, even beneath bandages, that seemed familiar. And there was something about that short, fat, podgy shape that looked so much like someone he knew. Fudd stared and stared, and then he hurried to a telephone.

When Grimstone and Jelly reached the hospital, they found themselves in a rather confusing situation. Almost everyone there seemed to be in bandages.

'Which one is Sennapod, do you think?' asked Grimstone.

'I don't know, but I have just spotted the Lightspeeds – all four of them. They must be here for the same reason. If we follow them, they might lead us to the Pharaoh.'

Professor Jelly was about to hurry away when he found himself challenged by the

sturdy, well-filled shape of
Matron Stubby. 'And where
do you think you're
going?'

'Um, I'm er ...'
Jelly couldn't think what to
say.

'He's with me,'
snapped Grimstone.
'Come on, Jelly, this
way.' The two crooks
seemed to have
forgotten that they were encased in
bandages and looked for all the world like
hospital patients.

Matron Stubby moved herself into their
path. 'You two boys are going nowhere in
that condition. Come on, back into bed with
you. Shoo! Shoo!' And so saying, Matron
Stubby pushed them towards a couple of

beds. The beds were already occupied, but Matron made the other patients move to one side. 'It's two in a bed these days, and don't you dare complain or I shall make you share pyjamas, too. Don't let me see any of you out of bed again! Is that clear?'

'Yes, Matron,' the other two patients agreed meekly, while Grimstone and Jelly ground their teeth.

9 Bandages and Bedpans

Seraphina Grimstone was getting crosser and crosser and more and more hot. She had been through almost every ward in the hospital, and not without difficulty. She had had to give blood at the Blood Donor Clinic. Then she had stumbled into the X-Ray Department by mistake and promptly had her entire body photographed.

She had also ended up lying on the floor of the Ante-Natal Classes, where she had to pretend she was having a baby and do special breathing exercises. From here she went to the Physiotherapy Unit, where she spent half an hour doing aerobics until she collapsed from exhaustion.

Gasping for breath, Seraphina looked around her, desperately seeking an escape route, and spied a door that was slightly ajar. Dragging her aching body through, she found herself at the side of the hospital swimming pool. Surely she was safe now? The pool was full of people and she wasn't wearing a cozzie, so there was no way she could be involved in *that*, or so she thought.

'Ah, there you are!' cried a jovial young man, over two metres tall and built like a rugby player. 'Wondered when you would show up.' The man turned to the bathers in the pool. 'It's all right, ladies, here she is at last. OK, in you go!' And without further ado he pushed Seraphina Grimstone into the water.

She was surprised, to say the least. She
rose to the surface, soaked to the skin,
spluttering, coughing, and trying to protest.
Before she could let out a single squeak,
several bathers had seized her and were
dragging her across the pool. Somehow
Seraphina had got involved in Life-Saving
Classes.

At the far end of the pool she was hauled
out, like a large, beached whale. The

bathers, who were all nurses on a first-aid course, gathered round, and at last Seraphina managed to blurt out a few words. 'Get away from me, you stupid clowns! I am not your drowning dummy! Look at me! Look at my dress! I'm soaking! I shall sue the lot of you!'

Perhaps it was more than just a few words. Whatever, they had the desired effect.

The bathers shrank back, leaving only the seven-foot rugby player grinning down at her. 'Sorry!' he said, rather too cheerfully, as Seraphina struggled to her feet.

Her eyes narrowed. Her mouth quivered. She took a deep breath and pushed him into the pool. 'Sorry,' she echoed, wiping her hands.

'I can't swim,' he gurgled.

'Good,' snapped Seraphina. As she swept

away from the pool she heard several loud splashes as bathers dived into the water. At least they had someone else to practise on. The door banged shut behind her and Seraphina squelched off into the changing room, looking for a place to dry herself off.

'You'd think there'd at least be a hair-drier around here,' she muttered crossly, but all she could find was a sauna, so she went and sat in there for ten minutes, until she was so hot she could no longer bear it. She staggered out with her clothes steaming.

The Lightspeeds were having better luck. By following the trail of cats, they had at last found Sennapod in the Observation Ward. It was quite remarkable how the Pharaoh attracted these animals. Nobody knew how he did it, but he did. The children had often noticed that, if they were out with Senny, he was often trailed by cats. Cats adored him, and the fact that no animals were allowed in the hospital was not going to stop them entering.

Crusher of Worms was the first to arrive, much to Sennapod's delight. Rustbucket was not far behind. An unknown ginger moggy jumped in through a window. A tabby mother and her six kittens hitched a ride on a passing trolley and soon landed up at the end of Sennapod's bed. In fact there must have been about twenty cats in all, cleaning their whiskers, curled up on the bed or sitting on the window ledge as if they were on guard duty.

There was one other reason why Sennapod had been easy to find. He was surrounded not only by cats but also by the hospital staff. They were pressing forwards from all angles. The Lightspeeds assumed that these medical people must be examining him, but as they drew closer they realized that, of all things, these people were asking for his autograph. He was sitting up in bed, looking very regal indeed. In fact it was almost as if he were seated on a throne.

'We saw you on the telly,' said the hospital staff. 'We recognized you when you were brought in. We think you look so cool.'

'Hot is the new cool,' the Pharaoh carefully explained.

'Can you put, "To Tracey, Love and Kisses"? Oh thank you!' The nurse bent forward and gave Sennapod a kiss on the cheek. He turned scarlet.

'You may come to my palace,' he told her. 'You can *all* come to my palace and be my handmaidens.'

'I don't want to be a handmaiden,' sniffed a male nurse.

'You will do what the Pharaoh says,' growled Sennapod.

Ben poked his head round one of the doctors and beamed at the ancient patient. 'Hi, Senny! Are you all right?'

'I am fine, Ben. As you can see, I am being worshipped. These people are my slaves.'

'Oh, he's so cute,' cried a nurse. 'I love it when he talks like that.'

Carrie frowned angrily. 'It's not a game. Stop playing with him. You all think it's a game, but it isn't for him. He thinks it's all real.' She forced her way to the Pharaoh's bedside. 'Senny, will you come home with us?'

Sennapod shook his head. 'I am going to get a palace. I must wait here. I am expecting it at any moment.'

'Senny, there is no palace –' Carrie began, but she was drowned out by a new voice.

'Oh yes there is,' cried Seraphina Grimstone, pushing her steaming body to the front. 'His palace is being built right at this moment. Now would you mind all going away and leaving my client in peace? I am his agent and if you wish to see him you will have to deal with me first.'

'Oh no you don't! That man belongs to me. I made him what he is today, a fashion

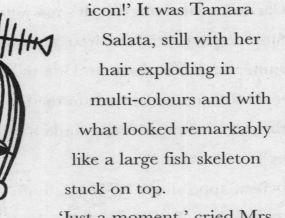

icon!' It was Tamara Salata, still with her hair exploding in multi-colours and with what looked remarkably like a large fish skeleton stuck on top.

'Just a moment,' cried Mrs Lightspeed, pushing through the gathering crowd. 'You can all go away. This is our Sennapod, and he lives with us and he is coming home with us, aren't you, Senny?'

'How dare you mess my patients about!' boomed Matron Stubby, appearing from nowhere. 'This man is in no condition to go anywhere. He can't move. What do you think those bandages are for? He is obviously suffering from a thousand per cent burns, two broken legs, two broken arms, cracked ribs, cracked head, cracked mind and I believe he has a dangerous pimple somewhere. That man stays here!'

And then a chilling command sent shivers through the entire hospital. 'Nobody move!' bellowed Grimstone, from behind the gathering crowd. 'Or the fat nurse gets it!'

A cry of horror went up and everyone turned round at this new development. Somewhere in the ward Grimstone and Jelly had found a nurse's uniform, and now Jelly was

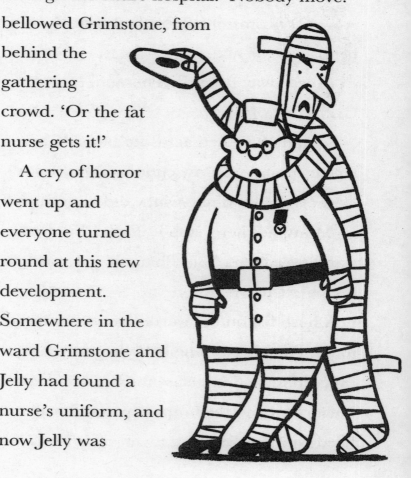

wearing it. Grimstone had one arm round Jelly's throat and was pretending to threaten him. 'Don't come any closer or I shall use this!'

There was another cry of horror from the crowd as Grimstone flourished a large bedpan in the air.

'Move away from the Pharaoh,' Grimstone ordered.

Seraphina rushed across to her son, her face beaming. 'Oh my cutie-pie, you're so clever. Who's a dinky-winky diddums, then?'

'Mum, not here, stop it. Right! Everyone stand over there. You, Pharaoh, get yourself over here, now!'

A hush fell on the ward. Everyone turned to the Pharaoh as if he held the answer to everything ... and that was when the doors burst open and the hospital was suddenly filled with policemen.

10 Doing the Pharaoh

'Arrest those men with all the bandages!' yelled Petty Officer Fudd. He did not seem to have noticed that almost everyone on the ward was covered in bandages, either because there was something genuinely wrong with them or because they were following the latest fashion trend.

Twenty policemen raced round the ward, waving handcuffs at everyone in bandages. A chorus of 'I arrest you in the name of the law!' went up. This was quickly followed by a rather mumbled chorus of 'Oh, sorry, wrong one.'

Five minutes later the policemen still hadn't actually arrested anyone, and they stood, scratching their heads, in the middle of the ward, their handcuffs dangling uselessly at their sides, gazing with increasing bewilderment at eighteen patients, all dressed from head to toe in bandages. One policeman was brave enough to ask Officer Fudd exactly which two men he wanted arrested.

Fudd had no problem with this. He had never forgiven Grimstone and Jelly for trying to turn him into a giant cake. He pointed out the short fat mummy and the one with the large thin nose. The policemen pounced.

Fudd ambled slowly across to the two men as they struggled in the arms of the police. 'Well, well,' he said. 'So now you are disguising yourselves as one fashion victim and a nurse. Will you never grow out of playing dressing-up games? And don't think you can slip away without being spotted, Mrs Grimstone. I can see you. Put the 'cuffs on her, Sergeant, and let's take them away.'

Fudd would have left at once, only half the policemen were hanging back, trying to get Sennapod's autograph.

'Love those bandages,' said one. 'I've got my own set at home. Versace – they're the bizz.'

'I've got some of that fabulous eyeliner,' said another, 'with glitter in it. I'm going clubbing tonight. You've changed our lives, Mr Pharaoh.' A loud chorus of approval came from the other policemen.

The Lightspeeds could not believe this display of enthusiasm. But even as they were leaving the hospital they began to realize that Sennapod's appearance on television had indeed sparked off a new trend. There were more and more people out on the street, all wrapped up and trailing bandages, women *and* men. They had rouge on their cheeks. They wore thick black eyeliner. Some had perfumed candles stuck to their heads, just like the Ancient Egyptians used to have.

And they all danced the 'Pharaoh'. That is what the new dance had been called, in Sennapod's honour.

Everywhere people were doing the Pharaoh, twisting their bodies into strange shapes and making those odd, hen-pecking movements with their heads.

The fame might have gone to Sennapod's head. After all, he already had a huge belief in his own importance. But he was strangely quiet on the way home, sitting in the back of the ice-cream van. Crusher of Worms and Rustbucket both sat on his lap, purring quietly, while Carrie and Ben fussed around the ancient Pharaoh, making sure he was all right.

'Do you feel ill, Senny? You've had a bad day.'

Sennapod shook his head. He closed his eyes for a moment, then opened them and turned to Carrie. 'I am a fool,' he said.

'Wow!' murmured Ben. 'You must be ill! You'd never say something like that normally!'

'I'm sorry,' the Pharaoh added stiffly. These were difficult words for him to speak. Pharaohs did not normally apologize to anyone. 'I was tricked by that foul woman whose heart shall be squeezed between two elephants and whose body shall rot in a snake pit for a million years. I left the only people who have ever truly cared for me, who looked after me. Please accept my apology.'

Carrie looked straight at Sennapod. His face was so, so ancient, and from such a strange and different world. But under all that pomp and bluster was an ordinary human being, a real human being. On impulse she put a hand to the Pharaoh's cheek and held it there gently.

A smile broke out on Senny's crinkled face. 'You are a true handmaiden of the Pharaoh,' he declared.

'No, I'm not, Senny. I'm not your handmaiden at all, and neither is Mum. We've told you that before. You do your own ironing and you scrub your own back. We're not worms either, or frogs or beetles or whatever else you like to call us.'

'A true friend, maybe?' suggested the Pharaoh, and Carrie smiled.

'That will do nicely.'

It was not all good news, though. The Lightspeeds had a nasty shock waiting for them when they got home. They had been burgled. They could not believe the mess the house was in. They didn't know for certain that it was the work of Grimstone and Jelly, but they were pretty sure. It was exactly the sort of thing the two crooks would have done.

'They must have been after the map again,' said Ben, turning to Sennapod. 'It's a good thing it's safe. It *is* safe, isn't it, Senny?'

The Pharaoh nodded. 'I hid it months ago. It is somewhere nobody will ever think of looking. Now that I trust you, I can show you. Come.'

He led the way upstairs and into the bathroom. Mr Lightspeed's face fell. 'Oh, not again! I'd almost finished redecorating this after that business with the shower. Those robbers have trashed the place!'

However, Mr Lightspeed's despair was not nearly as painful as Sennapod's. He was staring in horror at the blank space on the wall where the bathroom mirror had been. 'The map,' he croaked. 'It's gone! They have taken the map! It was behind the bathroom mirror!'

Everyone now focused on the blank space

as if they were trying to wish the map back into its hiding place. But the mirror wasn't there and the map had gone.

Sennapod sank to his knees and buried his face in his hands. 'I shall never reach my kingdom in the sky. Without my treasure, the gods will not recognize me and I shall be forced to wander the endless eternity of space, a nameless, homeless spirit.'

Mr Lightspeed reached down with a comforting hand and patted Sennapod gently on the shoulder. 'You think you've got problems! I've got this whole bathroom to redecorate – for the third time! Anyhow, I think this might cheer you up.' Mr Lightspeed took a flat, folded sheet of brown paper out of his pocket and passed it to the Pharaoh.

Sennapod recognized it at once. It was the treasure map. His heart leapt from utter despair to boundless joy in one enormous bound. He was almost speechless, so Tony Lightspeed filled in the details.

'After you so kindly spilled paint all over my nice new bathroom I had to redecorate. There was paint splashed across the mirror, so I unscrewed it from the wall – and guess what I found underneath? Exactly. I hadn't got round to putting up the new mirror before those clowns came in and trashed the place.'

Sennapod rose to his feet. 'We must celebrate our victory over those evil locusts, for Jelly and the Grimstones have been found wanting on Anubis's Scales of Justice, and they shall be punished.'

Ben and Carrie looked at each other. Celebrate? It sounded like a good idea. But how should they celebrate?

'I know!' Carrie yelled suddenly, and she

raced downstairs and into the front room. A few moments later the walls of the house began to shake with the boom-boom-boom of her favourite band.

In the bathroom, Sennapod's eyes lit up. He led the others downstairs, and there the whole family began to slowly twist and turn and jerk their heads like demented chickens. It was definitely time to do the Pharaoh.

Ask Jeremy

Of all the books you have written, which one is your favourite?

I loved writing both **KRAZY KOW SAVES THE WORLD – WELL, ALMOST** and **STUFF**, my first book for teenagers. Both these made me laugh out loud while I was writing and I was pleased with the overall result in each case. I also love writing the stories about Nicholas and his daft family – **MY DAD**, **MY MUM**, **MY BROTHER** and so on.

If you couldn't be a writer what would you be?

Well, I'd be pretty fed up for a start, because writing was the one thing I knew I wanted to do from the age of nine onward. But if I DID have to do something else, I would love to be either an accomplished pianist or an artist of some sort. Music and art have played a big part in my whole life and I would love to be involved in them in some way.

What's the best thing about writing stories?

Oh dear – so many things to say here! Getting paid for making things up is pretty high on the list! It's also something you do on your own, inside your own head – nobody can interfere with that. The only boss you have is yourself. And you are creating something that nobody else has made before you. I also love making my readers laugh and want to read more and more.

Did you ever have a nightmare teacher?
(And who was your best ever?)

My nightmare at primary school was Mrs Chappell, long since dead. I knew her secret – she was not actually human. She was a Tyrannosaurus rex in disguise. She taught me for two years when I was in Y5 and Y6, and we didn't like each other at all. My best ever was when I was in Y3 and Y4. Her name was Miss Cox, and she was the one who first encouraged me to write stories. She was brilliant. Sadly, she is long dead too.

When you were a kid you used to play kiss-chase. Did you always do the chasing or did anyone ever chase you?!

I usually did the chasing, but when I got chased, I didn't bother to run very fast! Maybe I shouldn't admit to that! We didn't play kiss-chase at school – it was usually played during holidays. If we had tried playing it at school we would have been in serious trouble. Mind you, I seemed to spend most of my time in trouble of one sort or another, so maybe it wouldn't have mattered that much.

14½ Things You Didn't Know About

Jeremy Strong

* * * * * * * * * * * * * * * * * *

1. He loves eating liquorice.

2. He used to like diving. He once dived from the high board and his trunks came off!

3. He used to play electric violin in a rock band called THE INEDIBLE CHEESE SANDWICH.

4. He got a 100-metre swimming certificate when he couldn't even swim.

5. When he was five, he sat on a heater and burnt his bottom.

6. Jeremy used to look after a dog that kept eating his underpants. (No – NOT while he was wearing them!)

7. When he was five, he left a basin tap running with the plug in and flooded the bathroom.

8. He can make his ears waggle.

9. He has visited over a thousand schools.

10. He once scored minus ten in an exam! That's ten less than nothing!

11. His hair has gone grey, but his mind hasn't.

12. He'd like to have a pet tiger.

13. He'd like to learn the piano.

14. He has dreadful handwriting.

And a half . . . His favourite hobby is sleeping. He's very good at it.

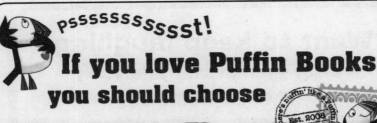